# AWAY
# WE GO!
by Rebecca
Kai Dotlich
pictures by
Dan Yaccarino

**HarperFestival®**
*A Division of HarperCollinsPublishers*

# How do we go from place to place?

# Sometimes fast, sometimes slow.

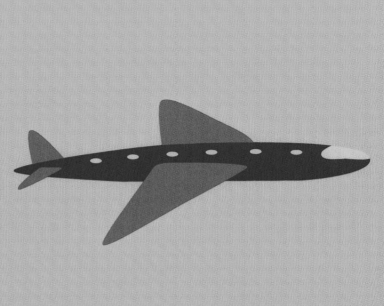

We float, we fly.

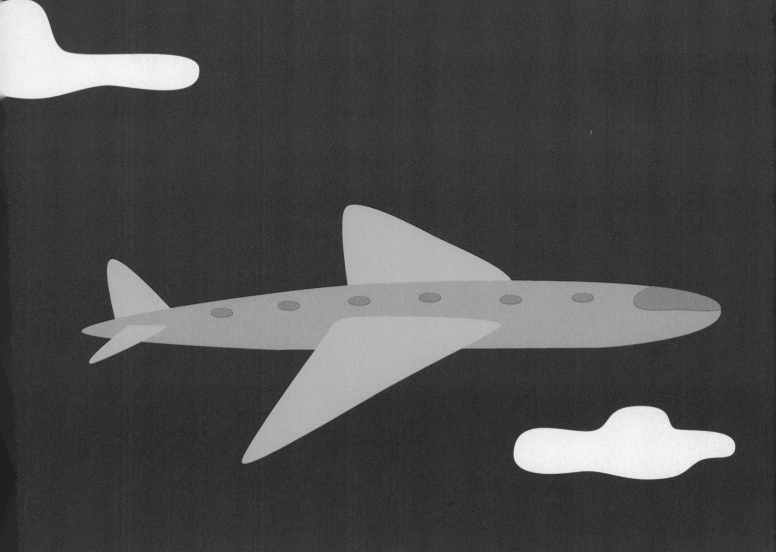

Away we go!

Taxi,

school bus,

sailboat,

horse.

A jumbo jet,
a car, of course!

**Ready to go?**

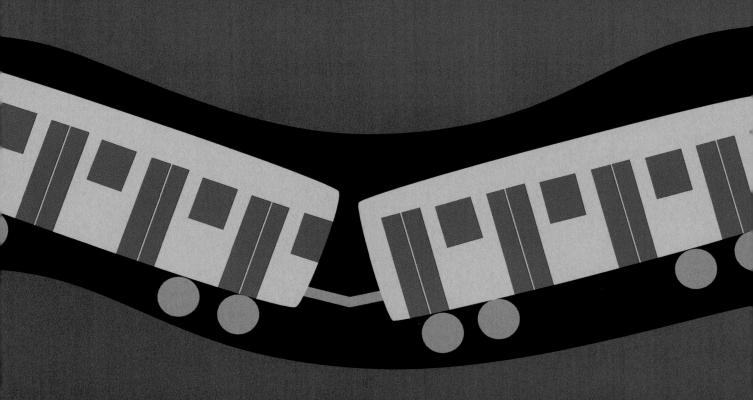

Let's go, by golly!

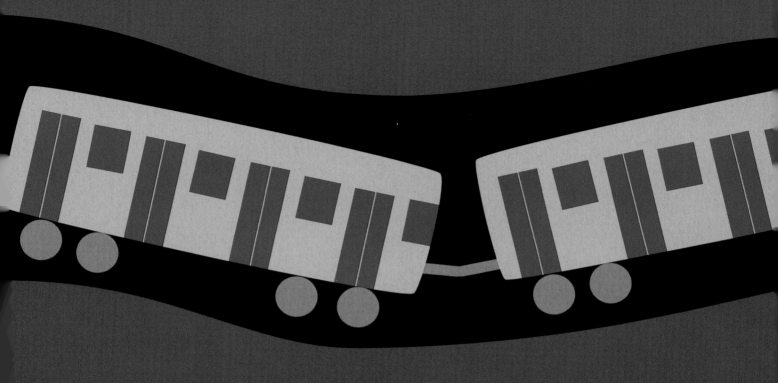

**On a subway, on a trolley.**

**Wagon,**

**wheelchair,**

**cable car,**

train.

**A ship,**

**a sled,**

**a bike,**

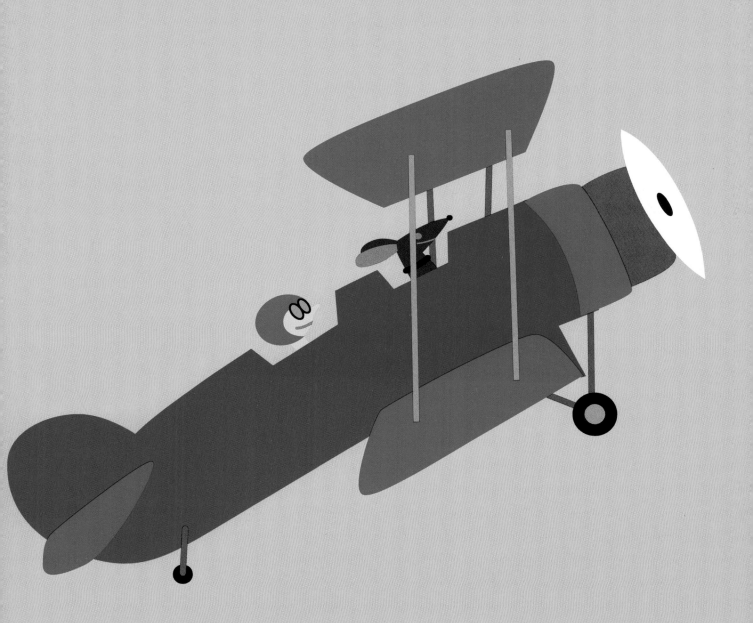

**a plane.**

## Sometimes fast, sometimes slow.